piano rats

by Franki Elliot

"Sometimes I run across a poem that makes me second guess my opinion on poetry. It could be a line in the poem that impresses me. Or a person in the poem that makes me wonder what he'd be like in another situation. Or a relationship that makes me want to know if it worked out. Or a memory I have while reading the poem. For me, *Piano Rats* by Franki Elliot had all of the above."

Shamontiel L. Vaughn
Books Critic, Chicago Tribune

"The book is a collection of deeply personal pieces, arranged as free verse poems, though Elliot calls them "stories." And they do read as stories, the kind told around a kitchen table—or even, in the case of "Nothing," a recounting of a story that happened while a story was being told around a kitchen table. Most of them detail a down-and-out cast with unbroken spirits, people who predict early deaths but live as if they don't believe it."

Jonathan Messinger
Books Editor of Timeout Chicago

"The 44 pieces in Franki Elliot's *Piano Rats* are like the best kind of chance meetings—weird and unsettling, specific and transformative. They are Frank O'Hara meets Ellen Kennedy, "first kiss" meets "fuck off," "hell" meets "rainstorm," poetry meets prose, narrative meets lyric, trailer park meets city street. But they are also entirely themselves, places where you "remember who you wanted to be.""

Kathleen Rooney
Managing Editor, Rose Metal Press

CURBSIDE SPLENDOR PUBLISHING

All rights reserved. No part of this book may be reproduced in any form or by any electronic or mechanical means, including information storage and retrieval systems, without permission in writing from the publisher, except in the case of short passages quoted in reviews. All incidents, situations, institutions, governments and people are fictional and any similarity to characters or persons living or dead is strictly coincidental.

Published by Curbside Splendor Publishing, Inc.,
Chicago, Illinois in 2011.

Fourth Edition

Copyright © 2011 by Sharyn Goldyn.

Library of Congress Control Number: 2011939708

ISBN 978-0-9834228-3-9

Designed by Shawn Stucky
Cover art by Shawn Stucky (© 2011)
Author Photograph by Stephanie Bassos (© 2012)
Manufactured in the United States of America

www.curbsidesplendor.com

This book is most obviously dedicated to someone I used to know...

Also, a very special thanks to Shawn Stucky

Blue Jeans	9
One Wish	10
Salesman	11
Multiple Personality Disorder	12
Who's Counting?	13
Heaven	16
Poetic Memory	17
Miss In Polish	19
Everclear	20
Snake	21
With An Obsessive Compulsive	22
1/2	25
Not Returned	26
Giving Thanks	28
Mermaid	30
Nothing	31
Wrong About Death	32
2 a.m. Breakfast	33
Easy Boy	34
It Only Takes Two Days To Fall In Love	35
Cleansing	36
Used	38

Flash Back:	39
Tiger Lily	40
The Coldest Person I've Ever Met	41
Milwaukee	43
Letter	44
Piano Rats	45
Week Negative One	46
Nobody	47
36B	48
I Thought We Were The Same Person	49
Run On Sentence	50
Slow Process	51
BK	52
Bull Dyke	53
I Hate Winter	54
Damen Ave	57
Your Latest Composition	58
And None Of Us Reply.	60
7 Hour Kiss	62
Maria	64
Sweet Disappointment	66
American Poetry Can't Breathe	67

Blue Jeans

The lady on the bus told me she met the Holy Spirit
and he was wearing blue jeans.
I don't know why she's telling me this
cause everybody knows

I

can't

keep

a

fucking secret.

One Wish

He called me up,
it was 11:11 p.m.,

and said,
"Every time I look at a clock at this time
I make a wish. Do you want to know what I wish for?"

What do you wish for?

"A Champion."

Not money, not fame,
not for his mother to be alive again:
A CHAMPION.

And now every time I look at the clock
and it strikes 11:11, I wish for one too.

Salesman

He said, "I'm not the person you knew before:
I'm a Christian now."

He said it as if everything we did
when we were kids was a sin.

He said it
as if everything anyone does is a sin.

And I get it.
He felt cheated out of his childhood,
he was always so goddamned shy.

Things happened to him that weren't
supposed to happen to a child.

And I get it,
wanting to be a better person.
I want to be a better person too.

But being sixteen and kissing in his garage,
marred and tangled with insecurity.

I felt like that was more sacred,
more beautiful than any religion
a used car salesman could teach us.

Multiple Personality Disorder

I remember your mother:
she had sixteen different personalities
and got arrested because she thought she was a trucker,
swearing like a sailor one night at the bar.

And I remember your father with his trailer and boxes
of blow up dolls and dildos beneath his cot.

And I remember you with ripped pages from books
plastered about your walls and quiet green eyes:

the words devastatingly beautiful and ice cream dripping
on the sidewalk still come to mind.

You were the smartest one in Philosophy
but passed notes asking to see my tits.

It was all because your Jehovah's Witness
girlfriend was cheating on you.

I'm not gonna lie,
I always thought that was most sincere.

You told me she's okay now,
she only has one personality:
a neurotic mother who smokes too much.

And your father grew a beard to his waist,
moved to the mountains and shot himself,
and you said something about wanting to join the army.

I said I wanted to sell roses in another language
on the corner of a cobblestone street
or you know, be a writer.

But you said, you can't be both, darling,
we aren't that lucky.

Who's Counting?

She called me up, didn't say hi,
just said "I need you to help me with my list."

We had done this before,
on 16th Street,
over blueberry crepes at an outdoor cafe.

We weren't paying attention,
and my purse was stolen by a violinist who got
just a little too close.

I lost everything:
my wallet, my keys, self-identity.

Two days left in that damn city and
we had to break into my one hundred year old house,
the window crashing on her hands.

I wasn't old enough but I snuck into the bar anyway
while she left in a taxicab crying.

Tonight, over the phone,
she reads off each name on her list
and asks me if I can think of anyone else.
I am surprised that I know almost every single
one of her lovers.

It makes me feel like a good friend.
It makes me feel like maybe I know too much.

We have a strange, desperate history
but I always say growing up together is a beautiful thing.

I mention one or two more,
we try and think.

This is bad, we decide.
This is very bad when you can't remember.

"Well, what about me?" I say.
It had been awhile since we'd sat together in San Francisco.

I pull out a paper and a green marker because
I can't find a pen and say,

"You help me do mine."
But she doesn't know most of them
because I had moved and moved again.

Easily, I remember every single one of them in order.
I have only had one one night stand and I decided
that it doesn't count. Or maybe I had three or five.

There are rules
for what counts and what doesn't,
or at least there should be.

She and I, we share a name on our list.
It makes us laugh and cringe all at the same time.
He was my first, he was her second.

"Thank god he wasn't both of our firsts," she says.
And he reminded me of a dial tone,
a flat line, a shade of grey.

The last time we saw him,
he bought everyone shots and
french-kissed a boy at a leather bar.

In the scheme of things,
we aren't sure if our number
is high or low,
so I ask around.

My sister, who lost her virginity on a tanning bed,
said she's at about fifteen. "About."

My writer friend, he says,
"Maybe a little over a hundred
but I don't really think it's any of your business."

Holy Mother of God.
I was his thirty-eighth and they say romance is dead.

One guy sheepishly says four,
one girl says ten.

And Modesto, he's engaged to a virgin now
but he won't stop talking to me.

All I can really say is:
Too many to count.
Too few to mention.

Heaven

He comes to the video store every day
asking if they have windows he can wash,
he'll sweep the floors, anything at all?

They all know his name even if they don't want to,
they're kind to him while they laugh behind his back.

We've all known him for years now,
we ate our hot dogs and spinach dip
at picnic tables while he told us about the lives
of Ted Bundy and Jack the Ripper.

These days he lives in the halfway house down the street,
talks too loud about Dr. Kevorkian,
has a cat named Berkowitz

but everyone, EVERYONE agrees:
he would never hurt a soul.

He couldn't.
He wouldn't.

He's completely earnest when he turns to you,
Windex and paper towels in hand,

and says,
  "Do you think Richard Speck is in heaven?"

Poetic Memory

I'm walking down the street when a boy in fluorescent pink
pants on a 1971 Schwinn Cruiser slows down,
stares at me and says,

"Have you ever seen anyone die?"

And I think of you, of course.

"Forty-Four Cents," you said.
"The day we broke up, I saw a man get hit by a bus and die.

"I watched the paramedics pick his shoe off the street
and thought to myself this is the biggest mistake
I have ever made.

"Forty-Four Cents is all it takes. You owe me that letter."

But I don't.

It's still here, tucked between two old records,
unsent, unread, unforgiving.

It began with a smashed rat on the pavement,
(I dodged our first kiss in the car, thinking I didn't like you)
and it ended with the words: petulant child.

Or was it the words fuck off?
I think it was the words fuck off.

Then: I give up.
The words: I tried harder than you.

Note: I've moved on.
Note: I've moved on too.

Edit: It should've happened sooner.
Edit: I can't even remember what this was all about.

There's this 1905 typewriter that keeps
calling me mercilessly serious.

I used to say it could only write love letters
and somehow I have learned to breathe again.
I'm expecting to see rainbows any day now.

Parting oceans. Cherry blossoms blooming.
Ice melting.
Birds on fences in rainstorms.

Whatever the fuck happens when
the opposite of falling in love occurs.

You said you know that red envelope is going
to make it to you someday but you're wrong.

I've fallen out of love and I feel nothing but relief.

Miss In Polish

My grandma can't tell you my name
but she knows I live in Chicago.
She knows I have a brother,
and he lives in Chicago too.

She adjusts her hospital gown and says,
"You tell them I'm not ready.
I'll show them.
I'm gonna live another couple years."

You drove me all the way there,
through washed-up towns and stretches of oil refineries.
Wore a nice sweater and shiny shoes even though my family
isn't the kind you have to impress.

I liked that.
It made me feel safe.
It made me feel like I meant something to someone.

Sitting in the waiting room reading
as strangers whispered grimly into telephones,
you said, "This is the perfect book but man,
is it miserable in here."

The hospital room is freezing and
the doctor stands with a clipboard,
asks her what day is her birthday.

She said she knows there is a four in there somewhere.
I know it because it's the same birthday as Hitler.
I don't think she knows that. I hope she doesn't know that.

And my grandpa has never held my hand
before until today. He has tears quietly running down
his cheeks when he says, "How's the violin, ponnie?
Still playing?"

Everclear

He took two shots of Everclear,
hid in the bathroom and shouted
through the wooden door
that I had used him.

This was months ago (the using)
I had forgotten.

So many kisses,
So many cities,
Of course, I had forgotten.

"You put the moves on me,"
he squealed.
His face, ears red.

I know, I said,
"What's your point? This was forever ago,
I know."

But it's the hypersensitive ones
that always say I use them
even if they can't keep their dicks hard.

(He said it was because he knew
I wasn't a relationship girl.
I said, I think it's cause you're a fag.)

He took one more shot of Everclear
and began to cry on the back porch,
talking quietly to a friend.

He said he thought he loved me
and we watched from the balcony,
sunburnt and laughing.

His friend put an arm around his shoulder,
said, "Forget her, man,
she's just an elitist little cunt."

Snake

There was that time I was walking up 24th Street
when a man in a tank top and cowboy hat
shouted at me.

He had a long, beautiful snake
stretched across both fat arms,
its tail flicking around his neck.

He said with the hint of a Spanish accent,
"Go ahead, touch her skin."

I touched her skin.

"I have been searching my entire life
for a woman with skin as soft as this snake."

He reached for my arm to test things out
but I backed away.

I suddenly thought of that time you called me hysterical
at 3 a.m. after you read the news story about a woman
in India who marries a snake.

"It's just so sad,
the whole town thinks the snake is God."

I said we all do what we can to feel closer to him.

But marrying your own God,
I can't think of a more dangerous thing,
no matter how soft the skin may feel.

With An Obsessive Compulsive

I don't have any friends but as I'm leaving I bump into a guy whose name I can't pronounce while crossing Broadway. He tells me as we walk that I am too American, too skinny, says he hates blondes and when I get inside his apartment he demands I take off my shoes and asks me a favor.

"Would you mind...could you please just wash your hands...?" he leads me to the kitchen sink, one hand on my back. When I try to use soap, he stops me.

"No, no, you don't have to use soap." But I do, thinking of my father leaning over me when I was a child, making sure I scrubbed for fifteen seconds. Every time I wash my hands I'm counting.

I dry my hands on my skirt and look at him.

"Just cause, you know, you've been outside," he explains. He sits at his desk and apologizes for the heat. He's dripping in sweat but still is attractive. I have barely broken a sweat though the heat index reached 110° today. He pulls my hand down when I reach up to bite my nails.

There are hundreds upon hundreds of records lining his walls, photographs all around his apartment, and everyone in them looks like they are having fun, possibly more fun than they are actually having. That's how it always is, it seems. I realize I have never taken a photo of a sad person and I think I would like to.

I look at the photos on his refrigerator while he pours himself vodka. "I hope you don't mind," he says.

In his entire apartment he only owns two mismatched cups, one filled with vodka and for the other, he offers me water. He opens his fridge and there isn't a single thing inside. I can't hold back my laughter.

"It's because the grocery store burned down," he explains, matter of fact.

He sees out of the corner of his eye that the blanket from his couch has fallen to the floor and rushes from the kitchen, demands to know why it's there. I shrug. "I must've knocked it over." He seems rather panicked as he folds it and tucks it back on the couch.

"I don't mean to be forward," he says,
"but it's much cooler in my bedroom…"

So I follow him. I can't remember
the last time I'd kissed someone.

And it is cooler. And he is forward.

After scrambling through his music collection for the right record, he asks out of nowhere, "Do people ever think you're stupid?" The question is immediately followed by an apology. "Sorry, sometimes I'm too honest," he says, pulling at my skirt. I pull away. "I mean, are people surprised that you read books?"

I don't know how to respond. "Yes, people do think I'm stupid sometimes." I try to bite my thumbnail, and he pulls my hand from my face.

He admits that us sitting on his bed is causing
him slight discomfort.

"It's because our CLOTHES have been outside,
WE have been outside…"

He explains that in his country and in other countries, if you aren't cautious of germs you die. "It's not like that HERE but still, it's habit." He's squinting at my thighs and talking nervously.

Now I understand why the blanket on the floor is cause for alarm, why he asks me to wash my hands and instantly I am self-conscious of the sweat running down my spine, the dirt under my nails despite the dish soap. I am suddenly nervous about the germs I am covered with and leaving throughout his apartment that neither of us can see, and I'm self-conscious of my saliva once he leans close and tries to kiss me. He leaves a little sweat on my cheek from his own face but I don't mind.

Weeks earlier, we stood next to each other silently at a concert in the back of a record store. I remember how borderline painful the performance was, two people with microphones and a bunch of objects making unpleasant noises. The show completely frazzled him. Walking next to each other outside afterwards, he had told me he could only cum when a girl chokes him. He told me he has only slept with two girls and one of them he didn't love.

Now, in his bed, his lips twitching, my fingers crawling toward his neck, he knocks me away quickly—almost shrieking.

"I wasn't planning on choking you," I say.

When I bite him he complains of the pain.

"My people," he says, his lips pressing against mine like a jackhammer kissing the pavement, "we are very affectionate toward our partners, we are more caring, more loving than Americans."

There's a half moment where I stop to think, what the fuck am I doing here? And then it passes.

"I never really liked skinny girls," he says, tracing his finger up my thigh.

Weeks earlier when he told me about the choking, I had imagined whips and chains, domination and pain, but when I unzip his women's jeans he is nothing but an uncircumcised child who whimpers in bed. He is my second Asian and once again, stereotypes aside, I am less than impressed. I tell him he should consider shaving. "Sometimes I'm too honest," I say and I try not to hold his pretty, feminine hands.

How long, I wonder as he falls asleep, how long after I leave before he rushes his bed clothes to the washing machine to rid his sheets of my skin cells and bacteria?

I wait for the sun to rise; usually I can wait it out until late morning, until the guy wakes up but this time I don't care about being appropriate. It's not yet 7 a.m. and I nudge him awake, tuck my dried up underwear in my bag and ask him to lock the door behind me.

1/2

At the bookstore a bum opens the glass door,
peers inside and yells,

"COWARDS!!!"

The man next to me is holding a Japanese cookbook.
He has gold-rimmed glasses and a wedding ring.

He turns to me and says,
"He's talking about more than half of us, you know."

I know.

Not Returned

The exchanging of things,
he says, sitting on her yellow couch.
The look in his eyes. Ah, fuck.
The look on his face.

A green hat, still missing.

Two framed pictures of a lobster talking on the phone.
Unopened face powder and lip-gloss.
Her loofah from the bathroom & overpriced lavender soap.

Really? You gave me back my soap?

not returned:
his heart, hers.

A toothbrush, he can't remember whose
was whose after all these years.
A Charles Bukowski documentary that made
me never want to read him again.

And books.
Some were his,
some were hers.

There's the one she wanted to read to him as he fell asleep.
He read it after they ended, alone, recognizing the lines
she would love.

He tried to tell them to her
but it was too late.

Her porch is covered in leaves
and she's probably going to cry,
if only for a second.

She always hated the fall.
The season and the vertigo.

He said he knew it was over because the last time
they had sex, it felt lonely.

Five love letters in five red envelopes.

The first one was about how they met.
The third about all the mundane things
she had grown to love about him.

The last one, about how they ended it,
tucked in stack of old records,
never to be sent.

Giving Thanks

He has opened the third bottle of wine,
and like three Thanksgivings before,
I have already been insulted until I cried.

So, I'm rifling through giant photographs,
ripping them out of a hardcover book,
trying to clear my head.

Half of the photos are of women rolling around in an insane
asylum: screaming, sleeping, clawing, pissing themselves.

The other half are photos of celebrities from fifty years ago:
polished, heads high, aristocratic.

"I don't even know who these people are,"
I say, tearing another portrait from the book
as he stumbles into the room.

He grabs the portrait from me, his body wavering
over the bed and drunkenly says,
"You idiot, that's Sylvia Plath."

Flips it over.
"And Kurt Vonnegut."

He tosses them to the ground.

He tears out one for himself, nearly ripping it in half,
Bob Dylan is on one side. Of course, I recognize him but
now he's missing his guitar.

The other side, he points.
"That's Ginsberg and is that Burroughs with him?"
He studies it for a second and moves onto the next.

Edith Piaf, Nina Simone, Richard Nixon,
Whitman, Nabokov, Kundera.
They all float to the ground like fallen leaves.

"Henry Kissinger!"
he proclaims, holding it up high.
"THIS ONE'S GOING UP IN MY BATHROOM."

They all slide from his hands to the floor,
and I scramble to study them. This can't be right,
surely I would recognize one of these people.
They are so important.

When he stumbles away,
I look in the back of the book,
there is a small index.

As it turns out:
Plath was actually a French model standing against a tree,
Vonnegut, a German scientist with bad teeth.
Ginsberg was real but Burroughs was just a plantain farmer
from the Great Depression.

He got them all wrong
except for the sad women in the asylum
because according to the index
they don't have any names.

And I don't care who they are.
They're going up on my wall,
their madness in frames,
all of them.

Mermaid

I was sitting on the steps at New Montgomery
and Market writing frantically on a McDonald's napkin,
ink on my eyelids,

when this man in a business suit came up to me,
ran one hand through his thinning hair, and politely said,

"You look just like a mermaid."

"Excuse me?"

"You look just like a mermaid."

I wanted to tell him that I'd been spelling the word "toilet"
wrong my entire life, that I might never be beautiful because
of the mosquito bite scars on my arms and legs. I wanted
to say that I have never had a cup of coffee but still worried
about teeth stains, varicose veins, grey hairs, and crows feet
but all I could muster was a "Thank You."

Nothing

"That's nothing!" She said, waving her arm at us.

We all turned to her in surprise. We were talking about a twenty-three year old who had nearly killed himself falling off a balcony while fucked up on crack and his year of rehab that followed.

"That's NOTHING." My mother repeated.

"I was twenty when I had to take your grandfather into rehab..." She set her cigarette into the ashtray for a minute.

"I was twenty," she repeated.

"Back then when they brought you in, they strapped you down and you had to sweat it out. You didn't get Librium or any of those detox drugs they have nowadays." She closed her eyes at the memory.

"When I dropped your grandfather off I remember he just looked at me, tears running down each side of his face and he said, real quiet, 'Please don't leave me here. Don't leave me here.'"

She shrugged her shoulders and laughed at the helplessness of it all. "What was I supposed to do? After I left, I just went out and got drunk."

Wrong About Death

He told me at about 5 a.m. somewhere between hell
and a rainstorm that she was going to die young.
"Not that young, maybe mid-thirties to forty years old."

I looked at him and said I don't believe you.
"I can't believe you."

It's been four years since we've seen each other
and he still never told me what happened those
nights he spent in jail.

Now, on my porch in Chicago in the rain,
he touches my hand and says,

"Honey, I'm never wrong about death
and I'm sorry you don't want to hear about it
but she's gonna die young."

He was right about his best friend, he says,
all the way in Los Angeles: they found her
in a chair, naked except for her socks.

There were two needles on the table, a bag of heroin,
a paycheck for $2200 and she told him a day earlier
she was doing fine.

"But I knew. I KNEW. I'm never wrong about death,"
he repeats. "And I hate to say it but she reminds me
of you…looks just like you, honey, exactly the same."

2 a.m. Breakfast

I said it first
but he said it last,
both of us exhausted at that 24 hour diner.

The lights were too bright for the
kind of night we were having.
The waitress, she kept spilling things.

He said it as if he
had just now realized,
as if he had read on the breakfast menu
some sort of hidden truth.

He said,
"I've been desperately in love with her
for seven years."

It was the most confident sentence
I had ever heard leave his lips,
even if the confidence was admitting
that he was incomplete.

In the cab ride home,
he held my hand anyway,
touched my knee for a minute,
both of us unaware of each other
and thinking of someone else.

Easy Boy

They all took the easy way out:

The artist who jerked off
the businessman with a cigarette fetish
for a quick $80.

Bette Davis, dancing with my grandfather
in San Francisco while he was still fighting
the war.

He said he crossed the equator seventeen times
in one day but never found a damn thing.

Jim Jones, that prick never
even drank the kool-aid.

He died of a gunshot wound
just like Richard Brautigan
and John Wilkes Booth,
and my son in thirty years.

It Only Takes Two Days To Fall In Love

My favorite love story was hearing that
the first time they kissed,
she immediately threw up.
The second time, the same.

He said, "If I was a shaman,
I would have looked back on those days,
never kissed her and saved myself years of misery."

"It only takes two days..." He said,
"TWO DAYS to fall in love
and don't you STEAL my fucking story."

And I know this all too well. The first guy who said it
to me was so drunk he hung up the phone and puked
all over the floor. The second guy only said it in a hotel
room after I had fallen asleep.

Two people? That's all I get?

Either way, things are different with me.
I need more than two days: I need years.
I need jealousy and masochism.
I need to feel so anxious I can't move.

I need after the fact.
I need "find another person after me."

People like to say it's never too late but it's always
too late, and we're not shamans.
We can't save ourselves from anything
that's supposed to happen.

We just have to let God laugh in our faces
because bad things aren't necessarily not beautiful.
No, melancholy is just beauty of a different flavor.

Cleansing

"I am going on a cleansing diet," he tells me.

He's sitting behind the wheel; the car is warming up. He turns the radio on and adjusts the volume.

"Green tea, lemon juice, sea salt water, cayenne pepper. Ten days. It's going to get rid of all the toxins in my body."

He reaches into his pocket and pulls out a key and a small bag. He dips the key in and lifts it to his nose. One paranoid eye side glances me. "Don't watch." He shuts his eyes as he inhales.

"Cayenne pepper? That's a bulimic's diet." I say, tracing my name into the condensation on the car window. "You're going to be shitting your brains out."

He tucks the key back in his pocket and restarts the car. "That's the point. To get rid of all the toxins in my body. It's CLEANSING." He turns to look at me. "You should do it, too."

I think about it and shake my head. "I don't think I really have many toxins in my body...not ten days worth."

"What about beer, cigarettes..." he says, pointing to the pack in my hand. It's his pack. I rub the palm of my hand across his entire window, erasing my name.

I think about it, though, and maybe he is right. I am not a healthy person, I am just young. I think of all the toxins that are unintentionally put in my body every day, then I think again...no. It's a bad idea.

"I am not going to shit my brains out for ten days," I say, matter of fact. "If I want to get rid of any toxins I'm going to drink green tea and eat some blueberries."

"Well, you're supposed to drink green tea at night," he explains, checking his eyes in the rear-view mirror. "And then sea salt water in the morning."

"Why don't you just NOT do drugs?" I say. "Quit drinking. Try that for a while? Forget the coke."

He turns the corner and his phone starts ringing. "Will you answer that? And besides I don't do this a lot. I just happen to be on it every time you see me."

Which was only twice, I know. I have only met him twice. Either way, I still am slightly concerned. We were both young and ahead of everybody else. We knew what we wanted to do with our lives. He was fucking it up.

I answer his phone just as he twists the cap off a bottle of Corona. "You don't mind, do you?" He takes a swig as he turns a corner. First drugs, now alcohol. We have been in the car less than seven minutes.

"Hello?"

There's a guy on the phone wondering where we are. I look at the street sign and tell him. I don't know this now but the guy on the phone who I have never met will end up being someone I fall in love with. Someone I may still be in love with.

He tries to hand me the Corona while I'm talking on the phone: no thanks, I mouth, pushing the beer away with my free hand. I talk a minute more with the then stranger before hanging up.

"You don't like Mexican beer?" He shrugs and downs the rest of it while we are stopped at a red light. I look at him and wonder if him driving me is a good idea but when it's winter a ride, even a dangerous one, is better than no ride at all.

"No, I don't like Mexican beer," I say, lighting up one of his cigarettes and handing him back his phone.

Used

We were sitting in the grass
eating lunch when he said something
about his girlfriend selling used underwear
for money on the street like cocaine.

Ten bucks a pop...
how cheap.

Flash Back:

You and me naked
side by side

(waiting for sleep)

the only sound was our breathing
when you cleared your throat and said,
neither loud nor quiet,

"I wish there was a God."

I didn't have to say anything
because I understood completely.

Tiger Lily

You told me the locals said you were the
most attractive man in South America.

That made me laugh really hard.
Maybe it's cause you got that gap in your tooth
fixed or maybe it's your tattoos, one for each
of your favorite books.

You told me you'd like to meet a woman named
Louise when they found your girlfriend in the alley
trying to buy drugs. She threw spaghetti at you on
a Sunday afternoon.

After that, your letters to each other
grew shorter,
less excited...painful.

And when you finally made it to Chicago
we didn't fall in love like we were supposed to,
I couldn't even get wet.

You avoided my eyes at dinner while my sister
shouted that I never learned to forgive my mother.

And I broke down on the wet sidewalk
because maybe it's true.
Everybody tells you to forgive
but nobody ever tells you how.

In one day, we made each other miserable
just like you said we would.

My last friend standing in San Francisco...pilot down.

The Coldest Person I've Ever Met

He hands me $4 and says,
"Buy as much Dr. Pepper as you can."

He won't let me come inside his room,
he just begs through the door between us.

"I don't want anyone to see me right now."

And I know why.

The bathroom sink says it all:
a broken razor, clumps of black hair
and brown drops of water everywhere, blood.

LAST night while stirring cocaine
in a martini glass,
always he uses a martini glass,
he told me why he's killing himself.

Like most artists,
he blames his mother.

"She had me when she was THIRTY-SEVEN,
she only had me to keep my dad."

He fishes inside the glass for a clump
and rolls it between his fingers, studying it fondly.

"When she died, I was THIRTEEN,
about to lose my virginity. She fell while drunk,
and the police took her in so she could sleep it off."

He takes his torch,
lights the end of the pipe
and inhales a huge hit.

There's a delicate silence before he lets it all out,
and I'm leaning against the dresser, watching him.

"She never woke up. She was dead."

It was internal bleeding.
She died of internal bleeding
and now he's got it too.

I was tired.
His story was sad. I had to take a piss.
I saluted him and said goodnight.

A few hours later,
I woke up to get water and
he stopped me,
half-asleep,
my bare feet on the kitchen floor.

"Hey," He said.
"Next time someone tells you their life story
don't just get up and go to bed. Hug them.
Tell them it's okay. Grow up, if not for me, for the next guy.
You are by far the coldest person I've ever met."

I don't know if you're alive anymore but
I swear to you, I'm still trying.

Milwaukee

I'm not quite sure what this means
but those late summer nights are
something I can never forget,
smoking cigarettes on the porch
thinking of who we would become.

For a week,
you carried my short story all folded up
in your jeans pocket,
said you felt sorry for the main character in it.

That main character was me, of course.

You were going to be a musician,
me a writer.

Now you're in Nashville,
I'm in Chicago.
We never knew we'd become no one.
How the fuck did we become no one?

But today I read a sign at the bookstore on Milwaukee,
it said: REMEMBER WHO YOU WANTED TO BE.

So I'm telling you cause I know it's autumn
and I know how much we hate the autumn,

Remember
Who
You
Wanted to be.

Letter

I sold my soul for twenty-four dollars
and thirty-three cents tonight.

You don't know what that means
but I know you're going to think you do.

I hated your poem
that you keep saying is a letter.

The one that showed up in my mailbox
with no return address and one blue stamp.

I recognized your handwriting:
it matches those margins of the Henry Miller book
I stole from your basement.

Your talk about T.S. Eliot, my nipples, my moan,
and the cocktail waitress I had no idea about.
Just thinking about her makes me want to vomit.

You loved my laugh when I read books in bed
but I can't appreciate it.

You can't wear lovestruck at the same time as cuntstruck:
it's unbecoming.

You said never tell a girl you love her.
I hate your letter.

Piano Rats

Linguists have pointed out that The Hopi have no word, no phonetic sound, no grammatical form whatsoever for what we call Time.

And he told me rats live in the piano. I can't think of anything sadder than rats living in a piano.

And my grandfather, he used to garden, play drums, smoke cigars but now he can barely open a letter. He sits quietly, hearing lost, so we can never be sure what he's really thinking.

And that violinist on the steps of the art museum said that this all goes back to Constantine and the gypsies, they each had one page of the bible that they hid in their chests.

And the other day a woman called and said, "I have to cancel my appointment. My husband, he has cancer."

And the Bubonic Plague, oddly enough, started with rodents and fleas. Something so small (something hiding in a rotting piano) and suddenly, you've got a 75 million people dead.

And every morning in the shower I say to myself, everything is going to work out. It is because it has to.

Week Negative One

It's almost my twentieth birthday, New Year's Eve.
The runway show was canceled
so I slept til 4 p.m., had no one to see:
everyone had flown back home for the holidays.

Desperate, I called them up, total strangers to me still.
They knew of a party, and we drove his shitty car
through the hills to find it.

"This is it," I said, looking at the address on my hand.

He froze behind the wheel,
his hair in two braids,
his face covered in scabs and said,

"Look at those people standing outside,
I can't go in there, I'm wearing sandals—
I'm fat, I'm ugly, my skin, it looks horrible."

Thirty-five years old, a grown man, he was.

And the bombshell in the backseat said,
"Guys, guys! Wait a second,
I'm gonna sing a song for you
and I never sing a song for anyone..."

(even though her secret dream was be a singer)

She took a deep breath and nothing came out,
another deep breath and still:
silence.

People with wine glasses chattered on the sidewalk with
cashmere scarves and silver ties but our shortcomings never
made it inside.

Nobody

He had two missing legs,
kept a fake one in the closet,
always had a carton of Marlboro reds,
a bottle of whiskey.

He had two sons who grew up to be doctors,
a four-foot redheaded wife
who we all hear was a firecracker.

On Wednesdays,
we would play in the basement
while the old lesbians down the street
came over to complain over boxes of Fig Newtons.

We don't remember him saying much;
just remember the rotary phones,
green and red, we played with while they drank upstairs.

In the end,
all that was left of him
was a war prayer of sorts:
a box full of medals,
dusty patches and gold buttons
we pinned to our coats and
fake camouflage t-shirts from the surplus store.

I'm not even sure they were his
but I knew such honors were beyond us.

It wasn't until we grew up that I realized never in my life,
never in your life, never in most people's lives, will we do
something that will require being given a medal.

It's a thought to be both ashamed and thankful for.

36B

She takes a good look at my chest and throws a guess. "36B?"
She has the hangover of an Asian accent.

I laugh. "Not even close." She shrugs.
"I used to work in lingerie."

She looks at my ass and says, "Your waist is so tiny
but your ass is big. Real big." And I laugh. From anyone
else it would be insulting.

This is a girl who won't stand up for the elders on the bus
because of her 4-inch heels. She closes her almond eyes
and pretends she can't hear them, all the way through
Chinatown to North Beach.

She once called me out of the blue to say she had phone
sex with a stranger from the internet when she meant only
to say "Happy Birthday."

Now, she squints and pulls a pack of pills out
of her purse to show me.

"Fish oil," she explains swallowing a red one. "Good for
your brain. Take." She waves a pill at me. "You need some
memory...your brain always so scattered, honey."

She pulls out a green one. "This one is for energy. And good
for the sex drive." She smiles. "Not that I need that. Take.
You always so tired, honey."

I laugh and ask her if she feels any healthier taking all these
vitamins. She tilts her head, shakes her straight black hair
and frowns. "No, not really. But still, they good for you."
She swallows the green one while I laugh some more.

"I saw picture of you other day, you have very nice smile,
you should use it more." And this time I shake my blonde
hair and frown.

"What about you?" I take a shot, "34B?"

She laughs. "Not even close, honey."

I Thought We Were The Same Person

The day the lights went out, you and I sat
at my piano distorting melodies in the dark,
Beethoven and Mendelssohn shaking in their graves.

I lit a cherry candle and a cigarette while you told me
about the boy who raped you. I had no idea what to say,
it made me think of things like collecting candy at Fourth
of July parades or my purple bike with ribbons hanging
from the handlebars.

Later, bored, in the rain, streetlights dark, we found those
three garbage bags full of stripper's clothes and the look
on your face when you pulled out the massive pair of black
angel wings. It was a treasure amongst the sequined rags.

You took off your shirt (which was my shirt) and tried
them on, dancing while the rain rattled all our windows.

I liked your spine and your green eyes, your lips, your false
sense of adulthood, all that left over sadness, and right
there for a minute I thought we were the same person.

Run On Sentence

Apparently the profits
from my toilet paper
are helping people with disabilities

and someone told me Ben Franklin
invented bifocals because he was going blind
from Syphilis

and
at the bar on Monday
she told me everything in my life
would be so much better
if I would just give in and dance

but Chinese medicine says
I have a spleen deficiency
while Western medicine says its my nerves

and the last image I have of my grandmother
is her lying in bed, clutching a blue plastic rosary
and weeping:

almost a century as a Catholic,
you would think she would at least
get a decent rosary.

Slow Process

Last January,
you told me the only reason you weren't committing yourself
to an institution was because you could still write letters.
You said you'd know you'd finally lost it
the instant you stopped being able to spell.

I think about this often.
This assures me.
I always liked your letters,
they were always charming and blasphemous.

Now, I may have excellent spelling but going mad
is a slow process.
Like writing a novel.
Like discovering if you like men or women.
Or maybe something like buying your first couch.

And someone told me the only way to make it through
these rough patches is to remember to do things,
even if it feels impossible.

Sleep at night, eat breakfast in the morning,
sit in chairs and stand in line, wash your hair,
give birthday cards, worry about the weather,
go to work, the grocery store, watch television,
feed the cats and celebrate holidays.

Find something to look forward to.
Someone to look forward to.
Look forward to yourself.

Otherwise, you're not gonna make it,
and trust me, we really need you.

Or at least I do.

BK

We had just met her when she stood in front of us
wavering in my hallway on six-inch pink heels.

She cracked open a Miller High Life,
patted her weave, and said:

I birth babies. I birth babies ALL THE TIME...
Had six of my own, as a matter of fact,

and sometimes,
she said with feigned nonchalance,
sometimes the babies are DEAD.

We all stood there in silence,
unsure of what to say.

Who was this woman?
A midwife?
A back alley butcher?
A doctor?
A surrogate?
God?
Was she God?
Delivering babies to the ground.

Later on in that same hallway,

the shy med student
told me between sips of stolen whiskey
what it was like to dissect a human body.

"I'm not gonna lie," he said,
"No matter what, no matter how hard you try,
you will NEVER forget the sound, the feel of cutting
through human bone. There isn't anything like it."

Bull Dyke

When I was eleven years old he gathered me and my
two slightly older sisters into the kitchen for a family
meeting. We sat, faces dirt streaked from playing all day
in the backyard, staring wide-eyed at him as he smoked
two cigarettes.

A lifetime passed as he sat there, not saying a word and
barely looking at us. He wasn't old then but his long nights
at the hospital, the divorce, and life in general had started
to gray his hair and, though the top of his head was mostly
bald, the sides were thick like rain clouds.

He didn't even smoke the cigarette all the way through
before he lit another, sucked, and smashed it in the ashtray.
Finally, the "meeting" began.

His face was crimson and he looked a little sweaty when he
said with an adequate amount of space between each word,

"Your mother is a bull dyke."

There was another strong silence before he backed up his
chair, scraping it against the hardwood floor, and stood up.

He looked at the clock on the microwave and shrugged.
"Just thought you should know," and walked away.

All three of us girls sat there in a shocked silence. I didn't
know what a bull dyke was, of course, but I knew it had
something to do with my mother and her "women friends".
When you're little you know words like homosexual-faggot-
bull-dyke, but the meaning escapes you. It's just something
you're not supposed to say in front of adults and it's
certainly something adults aren't supposed to say in
front of you but I guess nothing ever happens the way
it's supposed to.

I Hate Winter

I unplugged the television. I unplugged the refrigerator.
I swept one half of the kitchen floor.
I've been counting my mistakes on the lips
of other women.

I walked to the corner and back again.
It was so cold outside I couldn't breathe.
I opened the newspaper and I closed it.
I did not see you in my future.

I have only told two men that I have ever loved them,
both were two years too late.
And there's this place in San Francisco
where you can get blueberry pancakes at any hour.

Outside, the sidewalk is wet.
My shoelaces are untied.
When the old woman waves at me through the window
on the corner, I turn the other way.

I can't look at anyone,
not today, not tomorrow.

The bus drives past me. The street is dirty, broken, and wet.
The funeral home across the street is cutting a deal for cards,
flowers, and caskets. I count my footsteps as I walk but I do
not call you. You do not call me.

At home, I never sweep the other half of my kitchen floor.
I heat up water for tea but I don't have a clean cup.
The tip of my nose is cold, and I keep looking in the
mirror while I cry.

I've been writing the names of every man I have ever slept
with in chronological order into a three-ring notebook,
and I somehow forgot to put your name.
I'm sorry.

They don't know this,
but I've been writing them letters.
Most of them will never forget my name.
Most of them already have.

Before all this I read seventy paperback books.
I drank vitamin C. I washed two pairs of jeans and told
twenty people my life was over.

My life is over.

I imagine a 4 a.m. bar with crooked strangers and dim lights,
you making small talk with a semi attractive girl while
waiting to buy drinks at the bar.

I never thought that one day I might miss you. I never
thought it would take energy to appear completely normal.
When we first met, I said I couldn't imagine us fighting.

I have not opened my mail since March.
I have never had a gin and tonic.
I always said the first person to break
my heart was my mother.
Then I realized the second was my father.
Maybe the third was you, but I'm pretty sure it was me.
The third person to break my heart was me
(and you).

I liked when you would talk in your sleep
while I stared at the shadows on the wall.

In the morning when you were downstairs,
I would wake up, wash my face and brush my hair.
I'd lay awake and wonder about your ex wife,
I'd think about which things in the house were hers.

You always made me feel so damn insecure.

I've seen photographs in magazines of the greatest moments
of mankind and feel short-changed. I've seen photographs of
women with high cheekbones and large breasts
and feel completely short-changed.

I have studied the faces of other people's children
and imagined what my daughter will look like one day.
I wonder if you can inherit sadness.
I worry that I've inherited sadness.

I have studied the faces of distant men in bars
and wondered about the size of their cocks,
wondered about their fetishes.
I wonder about yours and mine.

I have woken up happy,
I have woken up sad.
I have woken up every afternoon more tired than before.

My hair is freshly shampooed,
my stomach is completely flat,
and I have always wanted someone to fuck me
on a piano bench like Henry Miller.

I put strawberry lip-gloss on my lips to distract myself.
I buy a book I've already read from the bookstore down
the street because I can't think of any others.

I think of the blue light and the bottle of aspirin in your
bathroom. There's a fire escape and spider webs where we
once kissed, that concert with two thousand people where
you slipped your hand up my dress.

I'm wearing lace underwear, my legs are shaved, I have this
memory of my mother with a heavy camera around her neck
and gold earrings, I never saw her wear earrings before,
and I still smell just like the day you met me.

Damen Ave.

Somehow I didn't notice him at first.
Just like I never noticed the church
on Damen Avenue until the lady next
to me on the bus made the sign of the cross
as we flew by.

I was 500 years old,
the wrinkles on my palm said so,
but he was a 1,000.

We were strangers who made a half-second
of eye contact, a weak handshake at the bar,
and then immediately forgot one another.

Until one day, time moved forward then backward,
stars dissolved, and I'm standing at the steps
of that church, 2,000 years old and mistaken.

Your Latest Composition

A four a.m. bar full of people wanting to be seen
drinking, he leans in close and says, "Watching them
is a sociological experiment."

I'm not sure how this happened but I'm here.

"Tell me about your latest composition," I say, placing my
hand on his leg. He plays the bass and the piano but I hate
jazz, I hate him. This is my own sociological experiment.

I don't know much about him except he has hips sharp as
knives. (Yes, I remember last summer.)

He tells me that for every shithead he meets, he writes an
essay. He pats the Moleskine sticking out of his pocket like
an old dog that has been with him most his life.

I'm trying to think of when to kiss him. This time there is
no street corner, no rain, no taxicab, no moment. This time
he's a little less interested.

It's an art I realize, my brief interviews with William Foster
Wallace's most hideous men, an art I'm slow to master.
And I realize I'm here because the last one fucked off
to L.A. to be a television star. The one before that went to
shoot guns overseas, but that was of course after he fucked
my best friend.

Or was it the other way around?
I think it's the other way around.

At the 4 a.m. bar, my hand on his thigh, he tells me about
four of his drawings that a man in New York bought for a
thousand dollars a piece. He says the man feeds his cat too
many herbal medicines because he's lonely.

"His cat isn't even sick," he taps the table, a silver ring on his index finger. "These people, they are so fascinating." I didn't think I had to ask but have you ever been married? Do you have any kids? Are you a sociopath who is emotionally detached from women?

No. No. Yes.

He leans in close, points to his head and says, "There is always something missing. With everyone."

He has straight teeth when he smiles at his own jokes, jokes I'm not smart enough to understand. He wears those thick, pretentious glasses-greasy hair. Argyle socks with ironic loafers. He's the guy I've always hoped would one day adore me even if he once told me he couldn't fall asleep sober.

When I go to buy a drink, someone at the bar nudges me and says, "Wow, he is good looking." This happens to me more than one would think.

Last summer I told him "no" while glancing at another girl's earrings on the corner of his desk. He ate me out instead, said he always hated the word cunt. It will be another three years before he can make me cum and even then, it doesn't feel as good as it should. There's always something... something missing.

"Look at all these people," he says, glancing around the bar. At pool tables, collared shirts, laughter. "They think they are satisfied."

This is a sociological reality. Neurotic. Desperate. Depressed. For every shithead you meet you write an essay, well I'm writing one too. Those Moleskine notebooks are my only lasting friends even when they're empty.

I go to the bathroom to fix my face and when I come back he's gone. He didn't even say goodbye.

And None Of Us Reply

She takes it right out of a film but we don't know that:

"Loneliness," She says with her red hair,
"Is the human condition."

"No, it's not," says the Egyptian. He's lying on the
floor–stomach down. "Beautiful people.

"Beautiful people," he repeats, "aren't lonely."

"Yes they are," says the Brit, leaning over and massaging
the Egyptian's back. "Beautiful people, they are…what's the
word…empty, is it?"

No emptier than we are, I think, but I don't say anything.
I'm not a part of their story.

The air is thick–smoky, tastes almost salty and I'm sure it's the
cocaine they've been smoking all day. I never had, I never will.
I've seen them falling apart for weeks now.

They are all in love with the redhead. The Egyptian and the
Brit. Maybe I am too a little bit, can't be sure because love
sometimes is just another word for jealousy.

The Egyptian takes it right out of a B-grade movie.
He looks up at her green eyes and says,

"That thing about hope that you said…it hit me so hard."

"'Hope is deceiving, dangerous, desperate."
He puts his head down again, his face to the hardwood floor.

He clearly has lost all hope.
Maybe losing hope is the real human condition.

He clears his throat for a second and says,

"I deserve every ounce of pain I feel. I don't know how any of you can even look at me. I'm not even human anymore." And none of us reply. The Brit just massages his back, a cigarette hanging from his lips while she leans against the dresser, her own cigarette about to fall from between her fingers.

When I finally look at her, her face is wet. She asks us, her voice shrill, "Why are we here—all four of us, why are we here together? There must be some reason."

And none of us reply. Does there have to be a reason? Even though she is broken and full of imperfections and fucked up, I want to be her. I am in love with her tears.

I want to say that even though all four of us are here together, cosmologically fated or not, we're all independently fucked up and alone. I know what he means, to not remember what it's like to feel human.

But I say nothing, I am not part of their story.

7 Hour Kiss

1. He opens his palm and shows the coins. "I've got a dollar thirteen...can I still ride?" But the bus driver shakes his head "no."

2. (The bathroom walls say, "those birds on the fence over there...they are all going to die...")

3. The black drag queen on the bus, the one in the hospital gown, she thinks I'm pretty.

4. Piss drunk she tries to pass out on the toilet but knocks her nose, blood everywhere and still she is awake.

5. My right eye is tearing uncontrollably but it has nothing to do with this anti-war movement.

6. "I'm beginning to think I'm man-made," he says, brushing an eyelash from his cheek.

7. The bathroom—like all boys' apartment bathrooms, has the unmistakable smell of feet. Tiny curly hairs and yet another couch I call home.

7.5 Unfamiliarity has become familiar and instability stable.

8. "You really are an attractive girl," he mumbles, pulling his baseball cap far over his eyes, " I can't even look at you, you're so beautiful." Under his cap he is watching me. I return his glance but I don't feel a thing.

9. Sitting at the laundromat, the bums walk in and out, asking for our quarters, we shake our heads and feed them to machines instead.

10 The woman on the steps is weeping and the piano music floating from the window is slightly out of tune. She's looking into the Chinese donut shop, and she can't see the ground. She can't see the ground.

11 "The moral of the story," she says, waving her cigarette as we drive through faded towns, "Is you can't LIVE off of art. You can't."

12 "Everyone," I say, "Everyone has written a book but me."

12.5 He bites his nails when he watches movies. Sometimes, when he's with me, he bites his nails. And now, he bites his nails. He doesn't have any sort of answer and I don't ask him for one.

13 Three months of harmony and our goodbye is just a book you left on my doorstep and an awkward kiss on the cheek. I wanted so much more.

14 A paramedic takes both fists and pumps furiously on the dying man's chest, "Live," he sweats, "Come on, don't die on me...LIVE."

15 He calls me up all the way from San Francisco and he says, 'Why'd you quit?'" Quit? Quit what?' I asked, knowing very well what he meant. "Hard work, unhappiness..." He replies. I think for a minute. "Cause I can work hard and be unhappy in Chicago for cheaper rent." But it's a mistake. I don't know why I left.

16 "Seven hours." I turn to him, breathless. "How can a kiss last seven hours?" And I don't feel a thing.

Maria

"Michael sure can dance tonight," I said.

We watched as he slid across the floor,
linking arms with anyone and everyone.
First time I saw him smile in 900 years.

You lit a cigarette, turned to me and said,
"That's not his name anymore."

"What's not his name anymore?"

"Michael."
 Pause.
"He's Maria now."

You shrugged your shoulders as Maria did a spin,
a twirl. She swung her hips, squeezed her eyes shut
and beamed.

It almost surprised me except nothing surprises me anymore.

After that, it all began to unfold.
He was quieter than usual,
didn't talk to me for weeks
because he assumed I was into Jesus.

His hair grew longer, shinier,
his clothes tighter.
He avoided our eyes
and cried in dressing rooms
because of all the hormones.

But wow, he had some curves coming in.
He lost his stagger, grew more soft-spoken.
His eyes, they began to sparkle.
His happiness was beside the point beautiful.

She never re-introduced herself,
never mentioned the change of names,
the change of parts.
She didn't have to.

We all believed it.
She really was Maria.

Instead of pretending to be someone else,
he became someone else as we all stood back
and watched, completely envious.

Sweet Disappointment

It was something about the way we pretended not to see each other the first time we crossed paths at the bar before saying hello.

It was something about the blues singer on the record player, my legs stretched across the leather couch, his leg against my knees.

It was something about watching her in the hospital gown almost cheerful, silently wondering which parts of her ran through my blood.

It was something about the grapes in the freezer, the scar on my arm from sitting in the sun in his backyard reading. "I told you not to do it."

I did it.

It was something about holding hands with another person while I knew he was drinking a beer and watching in quiet jealousy.

It was something that was nothing, the slight instant of what could be fading into sweet disappointment.

American Poetry Can't Breathe

It's almost spring, I know because spring smells like cat piss.

Strangers nearly, you took me into your damp apartment,
clutched my ribcage, bit my skin as hard as you could
and took off my clothes.

We swigged wine, breaths hard.

When you went into the bathroom I thought about how you
were an okay kisser and even if you sell drugs, there aren't
guys like you in Chicago.

When you came back, I could tell you brushed your teeth.
You took off your jeans with a slow smile
(My god, I loved how skinny you were)
laid on top of me with a kiss and said,

"I don't want to do this."

There was a weak protest when I reversed it all,
retrieving my clothes in slow motion, a bit unsteady.

I was straightening out my sweater, your paintings
mocking me from the corner, when I said,

"American Poetry Can't Bleed"

"What?"

"American Poetry Can't Breathe."

We were quiet, now fully clothed, wine bottle half empty,
laughing at the absurdity of it all, trying to remember how
to act normal.

I looked away and said, "I've been trying to kiss less people."
You said, "I've been trying to kiss less people too."

Suddenly, it didn't feel so bad because that self portrait of you holding a knife in one hand and your heart in another is going to mean something to somebody and these words are a knife in one hand and my heart in another and they are going to mean something to someone someday too.

Or at least I think they will.
I really think they will.

Curbside Splendor

www.curbsidesplendor.com

Franki Elliot is a twenty-something author living in Los Angeles via Chicago. Originally self-published, Piano Rats sold out of its first printing quickly and was soon picked up by Curbside Splendor for an official 2011 release. The book has since sold-out by word of mouth and has been re-printed several times. Franki's favorite artist Shawn Stucky created the cover art and book design. She is currently working on her second book, Kiss As Many Women As You Can. The book is part of her ongoing live-typewriting project, where she goes around the country typing stories for strangers on the spot with her 1960's Smith Corona Corsair Deluxe. It is a co-collaboration with brilliant artwork designed by Shawn Stucky.